I couldn't resist the new sounds and smells.
Everything was different!

In every direction there was something I had not experienced before. The sounds of the birds. The rustle of leaves under my feet. I ran with great excitement.

So much fun!
I followed my nose to the next new place.
I did not hear them.

I did not hear them calling me.

When I returned it was too late...

Don't miss any of these other great books in the Lucky Laney series.

Flames in the Forest

Mystery in the Mountains

Trouble in the Town

Lucky Laney

Rescue in the Desert

Copyright © 2021 A. J. Moyer
Lucky Laney
Rescue in the Desert

All rights reserved. No part of this publication may be reproduced, stored in a retrieval system or transmited in any form or by any means, electronic, mechanical, photocopying, recording or otherwise without the prior permision of the publisher or in accordance with the provisions of the Copyright, Designs and Patents Act 1988 or under the terms of any licence permitting limited copying issued by the Copyright Licensing Angency.

Illustrations and Cover design by: Stephanie Chartier

ISBN - 978-1-63821-370-3

This is a work of fiction. Names, characters, places, and incidents are used fictitiously. Any resemblance to actual persons, living or dead, events, or locales is entirely coincidental.

www.TheLuckyLaneySeries.com

Inspired by the Pup Pub Members

Friends Are The Families We Create

Contents

Chapter 1.

New Friends

Lightning fast. The little green lizard scooted directly in front of Molly. It stopped for a second and twitched its tail. Like a flash, it scampered off and Molly was hot on its trail. Molly's nose was almost on the lizard when it suddenly ran between two large rocks, safely hidden. Just a tiny tip of the lizard's tail could be seen.

"Lucky lizard! Almost caught him." Molly mumbled, "I will next time."

Her black floppy ears drooped a bit, but she had a smile on her face. Her brown eyes were bright with excitement. She was a Texas Pointer mix, with short white fur and black markings. Her white tail stood straight up like a beacon.

Today, like most days, Molly is a very happy dog. That's because she is doing what she loves, chasing anything that moves.

Luckily, she lives where she is able to run freely. Molly's home is in the high desert forest that goes on for miles and miles.

This is Red Rock Country. Many of the mountains and large rock formations have names like Chimney Rock, Lizard Head Rock, Submarine and even Snoopy Rock. They are easy to find and can be seen for miles.

Hills and valleys are covered in bushes and brush, perfect for hiding lizards and rabbits. Sharp-needled cacti grow on the hillside. Red rocks provide cool homes for snakes and bugs. Higher up the mountainside, tall trees shade deer as they graze.

At the bottom of Molly's mountain runs a shallow creek with cool inviting water. Sometimes forest animals, like coyotes, foxes and javelina, can be seen drinking from it.

Lots of hiking trails wind up and around big Thunder mountain.

They twist over rocky ledges filled with slippery pebbles. Scary rocky drop-offs are hidden by Juniper trees. These trails are shared by hikers and bicyclists even on hot summer days.

Molly lives nearby and loves to explore the forest. One day as she was coming down the trail, she caught the scent of a rabbit. She took off running, dodging

in and out of the bushes, legs flying. Through the bushes they ran, over rocks and through the brush. The rabbit darted this way and that way.

Molly followed, excited and hopeful. "I see it and I'm going to get it!" she said. Suddenly, the rabbit disappeared and was gone, again.

After her long chase, she sat down to rest. Looking around, she began to feel uneasy.

Above on the hillside, in the shadows, another animal was watching the chase. Alarmed, Molly's hair rose, is it a friend? Or is it ...?

"It's a coyote," she thought as she sniffed. "But it doesn't smell like one. And there is no tail or pointed ears. That's unusual."

Then the animal above, barked and nervously paced around.

"It's a dog!" Molly thought, feeling instant relief. "I wonder why she is all alone?"

They looked at each other cautiously. Smiling, Molly made the first move.

She said, "I'm Molly. I thought you were a coyote. I'm so glad you're not. Want to play?"

As the dog carefully approached, Molly could see lots of gray and brown fur. She noticed she had blue eyes, floppy ears with black dots but no tail.

Curious now, "Who are you and where is your tail?" She asked laughingly.

"My name is Laney," she said. "Why are you laughing at me and asking about my tail?"

Molly's eyes opened wide in surprise and she answered, "I'm sorry, I never met a dog that didn't have a tail before. Let's be friends. Want to run and chase something?"

Laney thought a bit and smiled. "Sure," she said, knowing she was all alone and needed a friend. She didn't like being laughed at and tried to hide her hurt feelings.

"I'm a herder dog and not all of us have tails," she said. "My job is to round up sheep and cows. Sometimes I chase ducks just for fun. I love to run fast. It is one of my favorite things."

Molly laughed again. "I don't know anything about herding dogs, but I'm pretty fast too."

"I'll show her," thought Laney, and she took off running down the trail.

"Wait," Molly cried, "Follow me."

Together they both zoomed down the hillside, over rocks, through a dry wash, and up the side of the hill. Lots of red dust billowed into the air as they played and tumbled.

After resting, Laney said, "Molly, I have a sad story to tell you.

"A few days ago, my family parked our motor home at the campground. All the smells were so interesting. I couldn't help but to follow them. I saw a rabbit and ran into the forest after it. One thing led to another and I forgot all about my family. It was getting dark when I returned to the campground. I looked all over, sniffed everywhere and everything but didn't find them. The motor home was gone. They left without me.

"I'm not familiar with the forest and spending dark nights alone isn't fun. There are lots of strange sounds and smells. Once, something came nearby and growled. That scared the begeebers out of me. I crawled under a truck for the rest of the night and tried to be brave.

"Why did my family forget me? I'm sorry I ran off and didn't mean to be gone so long. I keep searching every day. I'm all alone and hungry. Lucky for me you found me."

Molly's ears drooped, "That's very sad, you can come home with me. I'll help you look for them. I'll also show you around so you get to know the forest and my friends."

As Laney followed Molly she thought to herself, "I'll never stop looking for my family.

I'll never give up. Never."

Chapter 2.
Playground

Laney stayed with Molly's family. The two were always together, ready for adventure. During this time they often visited the campground, hoping to find Laney's family. Always hopeful.

From Molly's house, there were many ways to get to the large campground. The first was by the narrow forest road. That was how Laney got there in the motor home. The second was to take a twisty trail through the high desert forest and follow it past the creek. Lastly, was the way preferred by the dogs, and that was to cut straight through the forest.

At the campground, Laney walked around to all the parked campers and sniffed for a familiar scent. "Nothing. Where were they?"

A man in a black hat and red shirt chased them. Thinking they were begging for food, he yelled for them to get lost. Laney's ears drooped and she left feeling sad as they headed back up the hill.

Laney and Molly left the trail and walked home on the sidewalk. Excited voices came from a nearby grade school. As they got closer, the dogs saw children running into the playground. Boys were kicking a soccer ball. Girls and boys were climbing on the monkey bars and swings.

"Let's go play," Laney said.

Both dogs ran through the open gate. Soon they jumped and ran with the kids. Boys and girls threw a ball for Laney and twigs for Molly. Playing kick ball in the grassy field was best. After the ball was kicked, both Laney and Molly were off chasing it. Lots of yelling and laughing kids were close behind.

In the midst of the fun, a school bell rang. All the kids suddenly ran into the school leaving the dogs alone on the playground.

Tired, Laney and Molly laid down in the cool shade to rest. They awoke to children running onto the playground again. Soon they were playing just like before. The girls ran to Laney. She happily licked their faces, glad to see them. The boys shared their sandwiches and water and played chase. "This is so much fun," both dogs thought.

Then a bell rang and the students went back inside. Quiet again, Laney and Molly settled down to

wait for the children to return.

A short time later, big yellow buses pulled up by the gate. School was over and all the boys and girls climbed onto the buses and the buses pulled away.

"Where are all the kids?" Molly and Laney wondered. No one came into the playground. No one to play with. Left all alone, they waited. And waited. Now the dogs were forgotten.

Laney and Molly just wanted to go home. But how? They ran around the playground looking for a way out. The gates were locked tight and a high chain link fence enclosed the area. They looked and looked for a way to escape. This didn't look good.

Their hearts were beating fast. "How will we get out of here?" they worried.

They circled the area and pushed against the gates but nothing opened. Then they had an idea.

Finding some loose dirt by the fence post, Molly began digging. Dust and pebbles went flying. Slowly the hole got larger and Laney took over digging while Molly rested. Both dogs had dirty paws and faces.

"Does this look big enough?" Laney asked.

"Hmm, let's hope so," Molly said.

Laney tried first. She scrunched down as flat as she could, then she wiggled and waggled under the fence until she was free.

Encouraged, Molly did the same. Since she was bigger, it was much harder. She flattened out. Wiggling on her belly, she crept slowly forward. Finally, relieved, she was so happy to be free.

A tuft of white fur from Molly's tail was still dangling on the wire. Laney looked back and felt lucky because she had no tail.

Chapter 3.
Charlie

One day, Laney saw a motor home like hers. She got very excited but it drove away down the street. "I won't give up," She thought sadly.

When not searching for her family, Laney loved spending time in the forest. Summer was here. Molly showed her the trails and best hiding places for creepy-crawly critters.

It was a sunny day and they were running around chasing rabbits up and down the hillside. They didn't catch anything but it didn't matter, it was just a fun game they played.

That afternoon they caught sight of deer high up the mountainside. Off they ran at full speed, in and out of the trees. Of course, after a mad pursuit, the deer bounded off out of sight. Giving up, both dogs trotted slowly back.

Laney was busy sniffing, her nose to the ground. Molly ventured off in search of something new. Following a faint new scent, she scurried away, not sure what she would find.

The scent was stronger now which caused Molly to run faster to investigate. Up and up she ran through the trees and bushes. She was curious as to what she would find.

Her yelping got Laney's attention. Molly was only a blur when Laney looked up. She took off after Molly, running at top speed. "What is it?" wondered Laney.

On the mountainside, Molly stopped at a cliff by a steep drop off. She looked down and barked.

Down below, lying by some rocks, was an injured man. Hearing the noise, he looked up and yelled "Help me, help me."

His blue shirt was torn, his jeans were dirty and he was missing a shoe. A dazed look of concern and pain was on his face. He could barely lift his arm.

Just as Molly was thinking how to help, Laney ran up. She looked and saw the injured man. Thinking fast she yelled, "I'm going for help." She quickly dashed away, back down the trail.

On her way up the hill, Laney had encountered a bicyclist on the trail. Maybe he could help.

He was wearing a yellow jersey and riding a black mountain bike. Just maybe she could catch him as he wasn't riding very fast.

Running at full speed, Laney quickly spotted him. She began to run circles around him. Loud barking got the attention of the man and he was quickly annoyed by this crazy dog. Laney was desperate and lunged at his leg. The cyclist almost lost control as he turned around and gave chase. "Okay dog, I'm going to get you now."

Laney ran fast and hard to stay ahead. Up the hill she went, the cyclist right behind her. As they got to the top of the hill, Molly barked sharply.

The bike rider saw Molly and then heard a voice. He pulled over, and looked down over the cliff. His eyes wide with surprise as he saw the injured man.

"Help me, help me, I think my leg is broken." The injured man yelled.

The bicyclist realized this is what the dogs wanted. Grabbing his cell phone, he called for help.

"My name is Billy and I just called the Search and Rescue rangers to come here," he yelled. "I'm coming down to you." Carefully, he began climbing down the hillside. Slipping and sliding over the rocks, around downed tree trunks, through bushes, he hurried. The two dogs bounded down behind him.

Billy rushed to the man and asked his name.

"I'm Jack, please help me. I was camping on top of the mountain. I fell down here and my dog, Charlie, is inside the tent. You must help him. Please find him. I'm so worried and he must be hungry."

Hearing this, Laney and Molly went racing back up the hillside, their noses to the ground searching for a scent. The thought of another dog excited them, and they were determined to find him.

Finally, after a long search, they saw a yellow and blue tent under a large piñon tree. They raced towards it. Laney was barking excitedly while Molly cautiously approached the zippered flap.

She gingerly poked her nose into the tiny opening and nudged it slightly. It opened enough for her to see inside. At first, she didn't see anything and was disappointed.

Something moved in the sleeping bag. Out poked a brown and black head, eyes wide open.

"Who are you and where is Jack? I'm very hungry and thirsty," he said.

"We're friends and here to help. I'm Molly and outside is Laney. We found Jack badly injured and now help is coming."

Billy heard the barking dogs and found the campsite. He unzipped the tent flap and reached inside for the pup.

"Come here, Charlie," he said. Charlie wiggled out, very happy to be rescued.

"Jack said you can live with me while he recovers. I bet you're very hungry. Let's go home."

Billy walked beside his bicycle, while Charlie trotted close by. Molly and Laney were close behind on the trail.

Charlie looked at Laney, then looked at Molly. "Molly," he whispered, "where is her tail? She looks funny without one."

Hearing that, Laney took off running as fast as she could go. "You can laugh at me but you can't catch me," she yelled.

Charlie laughed and said "You're right, Laney you are very fast."

Chapter 4.
Sadie

Several days later, Molly and Laney decided to visit Charlie and ran to his house. Charlie was in the backyard looking sad. Seeing his two new friends, his tail began to wag.

Laney said, "How's it going?"

Charlie said, "Ok. Billy gives me lots of treats and takes me for walks. He said Jack is in the hospital and I will live here."

"Hi," said Molly walking up. "Hey Charlie, want to come and play?"

"Yes," he said, "But I don't know how. I can't get out of this fenced yard."

Laney ran around the yard looking for a way out. The only thing she saw was a wooden plank leaning against the fence wall.

"I know, you can walk up the plank and jump over. Want to try it?" Laney said.

The pup eyed the long narrow piece of wood. "Easy- peasy," he said, sounding very sure of himself.

He walked to the plank and started up, one paw in front of the other. After five steps he started to tremble. That caused him to lose his balance. He slipped off the side, head over paws, all waving feet, to the ground.

"Not so easy," he grumbled.

"Oops, shake it off" Molly yelled. "You can do it."

Charlie backed away, shaking his head, "I don't think I can, it's too high."

Both Laney and Molly urged him and yelled "Try it again Charlie, you can do it."

He started up the plank again, looking very unsettled. He put one paw in front of the other. He was almost to the top when his back paw slipped off the side. Again, he tumbled all the way down to the ground. That caused the dogs to giggle, even Charlie.

"We know you can do it, Charlie, try harder. This time, look at me, and don't look down," said Molly.

"Ohhhhkay." Charlie started slowly walking up again. Eyes only on Molly. Suddenly he was standing at the top of the wall.

"Now jump" they urged, and over he went, joining his friends. "Yay, you did it," they yelled.

As they walked, they smelled a strong odor. "What is that smell?" Laney asked.

Charlie chuckled and said "That is my neighbor's dog, Sadie. Let's go say hi. She's older, but still fun."

Sadie, a brown lab, was lounging in the backyard. She had soft brown eyes, a roly poly belly and brown tail. She lazily greeted them through the fence and Charlie introduced Laney and Molly.

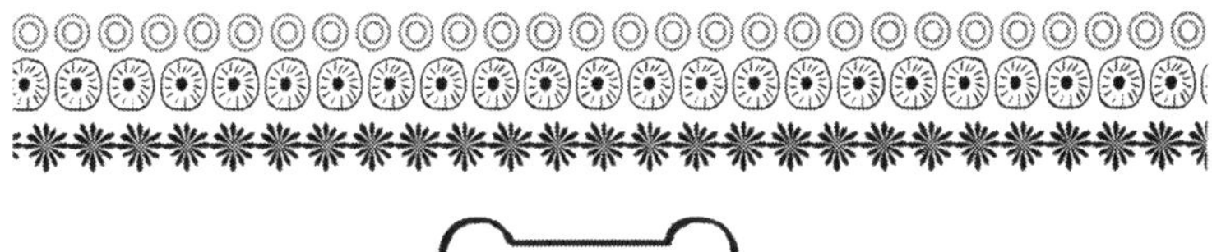

Laney told Sadie how she lost her family and was staying with Molly. They were going to the campgrounds to search again.

"You are kinda smelly, what happened?" asked Molly "I don't recognize that smell."

Sadie explained, "My dad and I went walking on the trail a couple of days ago. I went to investigate a large hollow log that had fallen. I stuck my head inside and saw this black and white small furry animal. I barked and tried to back up when I was sprayed with something stinky and warm. The spray stung my eyes and nose and smelled terrible. My dad yelled at me, took me home and washed me three times."

With tearful eyes, she said, "It was so awful and now I'm confined to the yard."

Laney, Molly and Charlie felt very sorry for Sadie. Molly said, "Maybe next time you can come with us."

Just then, a tall man in a green uniform walked out of the house. He was wearing a white cowboy hat and a shiny bright star was on his shirt.

"That's my dad," said Sadie proudly. "He's a sheriff and helps people. Hey, maybe he can help you find your family."

That made Laney very, very happy.

Chapter 5.
Javelina

Out on the trail, Laney, Molly and Charlie trotted towards the campground once again. On the way, they chased anything that moved. They moved quickly through the brush playing chase. Up and down the hillside they ran. Finally, tired, they saw the creek.

Laney was very hot from all the activity and happily ran into the cool water. Splashing everywhere. Molly stepped into the water for a few minutes. It felt so good. Charlie just looked. He didn't like the running water and went to find a cool place to rest. Tired, Molly dug a hole in the loose red dirt under a shade tree and plopped down. Laney played in the water a little longer before also settling down for a snooze beside Molly.

All was quiet except for the chirping birds and bubbling water in the creek.

Then a twig snapped. Molly's head went up. Laney scrambled to her feet, alert.

Walking toward the creek was a family of javelinas. Looking a bit like a wild boar, they have gray brown hair, short legs and a pig-like nose. Their eyesight is poor but they have a very good sense of smell. Busily looking for berries to eat, they did not immediately notice the dogs.

Then they caught a scent. Heads went up. They kept walking slowly while watching the dogs. A mom and her baby quickly backed away into the bushes. Several smaller ones also ran off. The larger ones were more aggressive. While they were larger than the dogs, they were much slower.

Laney ran toward them. She circled around, not getting close. She thought, "These are wild animals and can sometimes be mean."

Molly also jumped up, and ran toward the group. Barking loudly, both dogs were very excited. This didn't look good.

The javelina stopped, waiting. The hair on their backs raised, they were clearly alarmed at the dogs. They shook their heads back and forth in a menacing manner, tusks flashing. An aggressive javelina bolted toward Laney.

Laney quickly jumped away. Again, another dashed forward toward Molly.

Several other Javalinas snorted loudly and ran around, but the dogs easily dodged them.

Working as a team, Laney and Molly circled the remaining javelina while running and darting. They pushed the group back to the creek. Suddenly, the javelina turned and disappeared into the brush. They did not like the two loud barking dogs.

Charlie watched the action with wide eyes.

"Holy Moley, that was scary. They looked ready to attack. I'm glad they ran off," he said.

Laney and Molly agreed, very happy to have chased them away. They were relieved the threatening animals were gone.

"Let's go home now," said Charlie. "I'm hungry." Off they raced to home. But could Charlie get back inside the yard?

As they neared the house, they saw Billy. The gate was now open. He had unlatched the gate for Charlie to return.

Chapter 6.
Coyote

Laney often thought of her family and kept searching. The sheriff also made inquiries at the campground without success. That didn't make Laney feel very happy. She thought, "If only I could find them, I'll never run off again."

The summer slid past with lots of playtime for the three friends. Laney went splashing in the creek at every chance. She loved the cool water. Molly and Charlie chased everything that scooted away. The trails, hills and mountains were their playground. It was a happy time to run freely. But Laney still missed her family.

The leaves turned red orange and fell from the oak trees. As the dogs played and wrestled, dry leaves scattered and flew everywhere. Squirrels were gathering nuts and seeds to hide. Rabbits built winter nests and snakes disappeared.

Lots of activity was going on in the forest.

"Let's hit the trail," yelled Laney.

Molly and Charlie were already flying down the hillside. The deep ravines held interesting smells. It was a good hiding spot for many animals. Coyote, javelina and even bobcats had recently visited the area.

Molly caught an unusual scent and was busily following it. The other two were exploring on their own. Soon Molly was over the ridge and out of sight. Hidden by bushes and trees, she followed the smell. Her nose pressed intently on the ground.

The brush was thick enough for the coyote to hide in. He stood very still, eyes watching Molly. He wasn't ready to make his move yet. Head high, a low growl started forming. He had a hard mean look and his gray fur was blotchy from many fights.

Molly looked up and saw movement. Dashing down the trail was a large coyote. Quickly, she sprinted in pursuit. She did not like coyotes.

They ran deeper into the forest, past trees, jumping over the brush. The coyote ran down a dry wash filled with rocks and large boulders. He looked over his shoulder to make sure she was still falling for his trap.

It was hard running but Molly was gaining and getting closer. Suddenly, the coyote jumped up on a

boulder and growled loudly. Excited, Molly yipped and barked at him.

The wind was blowing and carried the sounds back to Laney and Charlie. At once, both took off running toward Molly, not sure what they would find.

Molly was in trouble. When she rounded the corner, she was blocked by two large boulders. The coyote was above her looking into the forest.

Coming up the hillside were two skinny, mangy-looking coyotes. They were headed straight toward Molly. Concerned, she barked sharply.

Laney arrived first. She was slightly up the hillside and saw the three coyotes. Charlie was still trying to catch up. Thinking fast, Laney ran toward the two approaching animals. She was ready to charge them but quickly changed directions. Veering away, Laney dared them to follow her. The trick worked and the chase was on.

Running, jumping, soaring over shrubs, bushes, and rocks, flew Laney. Everywhere, the two coyotes followed but never gained on her. Pebbles went flying amid great clouds of red dust. Zigging and zagging, they got further away from Molly and the other coyote.

Charlie emerged from the trees and saw the commotion. What to do? How to help? He hesitated for a second.

At the same time, the menacing coyote jumped down from above. It landed very close to Molly. Sensing Molly was trapped and couldn't get away, the coyote bolted forward, ready to attack.

Without another thought, Charlie quickly ran forward. He slammed into the coyote's back legs and began to nip and bite. Startled, the coyote swung around. That allowed enough room for Molly to move.

The coyote was outnumbered. Yelping like he was wounded, he leaped away. Running as fast as he could, he headed for the open forest.

When the other two saw their leader running away, they also took off. Over the hill went the pack, heads down and tails between their legs. They knew they had been beaten.

Panting hard, Laney returned to find Molly and Charlie.

"That was awesome," Molly said. "You both were great, thank you. We showed them."

Looking at Molly, Laney said, "You were very brave to stand your ground."

Molly turned to Charlie and said, "That was a good surprise attack, you were like a super ninja."

Still very excited, Charlie bounced around with a pleased look on his face.

It was almost dusk as the dogs started home. They walked slowly as Laney was limping on three legs. She had hurt her leg during the chase. Molly's head and white tail were pointed high.

Charlie was close beside them, his brown tail wagging happily.

They were happy and proud. Working together, they chased off three scary coyotes. It was a good feeling to have helped each other and they were now best friends.

Chapter 7.

Capture

After the coyote incident, the dogs stayed close to home. Laney thought of her family but was not so eager to go back to the campground.

One morning, Molly and Laney decided to visit Charlie and Sadie. The dogs quickly joined them, easily getting out of their yards. Together they ran and wrestled before finally settling down to rest. Once in a while their eyes would glance around, heads on their paws, just being lazy.

Nothing much was happening except for some loud black ravens fluttering in the piñon trees. They were very big and Laney did not like their beady eyes or sharp pointy beaks. The birds would fly teasingly close then dart away or sit just out of reach of the dogs, cawing loudly. They looked scary. Laney thought, "If I ever catch one..." It was fall and the pinecones were bursting open. The birds loved to eat the seeds out of the pinecones.

Soon, more birds came to feast and pinecones were tossed on the ground. Birds came from everywhere. They all wanted the seeds. They squawked loudly as they fluttered and hopped around looking for pine nuts.

One large bird landed on a rock near the dogs. Another came, and several more landed on the ground and street. It seemed like a hundred birds. The dogs stayed quiet except for alert eyes and ears. However, this was too good to resist. The birds were moving into the dogs' territory. Laney and Molly smiled.

The dogs jumped up as one and ran toward the birds on the ground. A cloud of black feathers filled the air. Wings flapping wildly. Dozens of birds flew quickly to the safety of the trees making funny cawing and clicking sounds. The dogs jumped as high as they could but they could not fly like the birds.

Disappointed, the dogs settled back down. Again, the ravens saw the pinecones and could not resist. Soon they were back in the trees and on the ground, eating seeds. They loved teasing the dogs.

Again, Charlie and Laney ran full speed at the birds. It was quite a sight!

Big black birds filled the sky in every direction. They scattered everywhere.

Whoosh, the birds flew over and around the resting dogs. This time no one moved. The ravens were annoying but all interest was gone. The dogs loved a good game of chase but they no longer wanted to play with silly nobody birds.

Molly said "Let's try the trail and not go very far." The little group of four happily ran off, forgetting all about the pesky ravens.

Lead dog Laney set the pace and soon led the way on the trail. Charlie and Molly were close behind. The three were ahead of Sadie, who was trotting slowly down the trail. They quickly lost sight of her.

Hearing voices, Sadie stopped. Coming onto the trail were two men in brown uniforms with dog catcher badges on the sleeves of their shirts.

They approached her slowly and said, "Well, what do we have here? It looks like a tired, hungry dog, lost in the forest."

"Come here and we'll help you." With that, they slipped a leash over her head and led Sadie away.

Hearing the voices, the other dogs saw what was happening but didn't understand it. They followed the men a short distance.

They saw Sadie being placed into a dog crate inside a truck. It quickly drove off down the street.

Where was she going? Why did they take Sadie? What was happening?

Chapter 8.
Rescue

Alarmed, they decided to follow the truck and rescue Sadie. Focusing intently, they started off. They stayed off the busy street and trotted on the sidewalk. Though they appeared brave, this was new to the dogs and very unsettling.

They walked and walked. Stopping now and then to rest, they stayed hidden behind bushes. It seemed they had walked miles and miles.

The cars whizzed past. Horns honked. Trucks and buses were big and noisy. The traffic never stopped. Still, they bravely followed the faint scent of Sadie and the truck.

They came around a bend in the road and ahead of them was the town. They stopped as one and just looked. Buildings and shops were on both sides of the street. Lots of people were walking on the sidewalks. Many were shopping and had lots of packages.

"Wow" Molly said, "it's a busy place. Let's stay together and try to be invisible." So they started forward, staying close to the buildings but away from the people. Mostly they were ignored. Walking single file, they could scoot around quickly.

Ahead of them was an intersection. A few people were standing and waiting at the traffic signal. Dodging the shoppers, Laney got separated from the other dogs. Seeing cars driving by at the intersection, she sat down to wait. A lady in a pink coat, arms filled with packages, was beside her.

Then something happened. Suddenly, the lady gave a loud cry as she fell forward. She went splat into the street. Her glasses flew off and packages scattered everywhere. She looked very dazed and hurt.

Laney saw the car speeding toward them. She quickly ran into the street in front of the fallen lady and barked sharply. Sitting very still and trying not to tremble, Laney protected the injured lady.

The driver honked its horn and braked hard. Wheels squealed as the car stopped directly in front of Laney. The spectators just gasped. It was a scary tense moment.

The driver was a young girl. She got out and ran forward yelling. "I didn't see you!"

“I’m sorry I almost hit you,” she said. “What happened?” Tears formed in her eyes as she looked first at Laney then the lady. She was very shaken.

Several people stepped forward to help. A policeman appeared and said he called an ambulance.

As the policeman was directing traffic around the group, a news van drove up and stopped. Out jumped a newspaper reporter with his video camera filming the commotion. Others were also taking photos and videos with their cell phones. Everyone was talking at once. It was very noisy.

Hearing the approaching ambulance with its siren blaring, Laney knew help was on its way. She turned and glanced at the lady still lying in the street. Someone was talking to her. Getting more anxious and nervous with all the people around her, Laney quietly backed away to find Molly and Charlie.

The two dogs were huddled beside a shop looking very alert when Laney found them.

Molly said, "Let's get away from here, we still need to find Sadie."

The sun was going down when they reached the end of town.

"I see the truck parked in front of this building, let's look inside," said Laney . "This may be where Sadie is."

Charlie looked wide eyed at the large grey building, "Is Sadie in jail?" he asked.

Just then the two men came out, locked the door behind them and drove off.

The dogs heard Sadie bark and they barked back hoping she could hear them. Looking around, things looked bleak for rescuing Sadie.

Molly said, "We'll have to wait until morning and figure out something."

They were very tired and hungry. They wanted to stay close and not go anywhere, so they huddled together at the rear of the building. No one complained, not even Charlie. They quickly fell asleep.

The sun was shining brightly when they woke up. Hearing the truck and men return, the dogs got up. The shelter door was open when another car quickly drove up and parked.

"That's the sheriff," Molly said.

The sheriff got out. Seeing the two men, he excitedly told them his dog was lost. She hadn't come home and he was very worried.

The men told him how they found a brown lab who looked lost and lonely. She was wandering around in the forest so they brought her to the shelter.

They heard a bark from inside. "Why that's Sadie," the sheriff said. "She's here and safe. Let's get her out of that crate. I'm taking her home."

Hearing the sheriff's voice, the three dogs walked to the open doorway and looked inside.

The sheriff saw them and was very surprised. "Well, well, what are you doing here? Did you come to rescue Sadie too?

"I'm taking you all home," he said. He put Sadie in the front seat and the other three rode in the back seat of the sheriff car feeling very special.

After delivering them home, he said "I think you should all stay home for a while and not get into any more trouble."

Chapter 9
Family

A few days later, the sheriff got a phone call from a very excited couple.

They explained they had just read an article in the newspaper. It was about a mystery dog saving an injured lady. The photo of the dog looked just like their lost dog. She disappeared from the campground several months ago. Does the sheriff know this dog?

The sheriff told them to meet at his office and he would try to help. He had heard the story of a dog saving a lady but had not seen the newspaper article. Finding the front page of the paper, he stared at the photo and his mouth fell open in surprise.

"That dog looks just like Laney. I think she's the mystery dog," he exclaimed.

When the couple arrived, he was ready to take them to see the dog. He cautioned this may not be their lost dog.

Molly and Laney were in the backyard when the sheriff's car drove up. They mostly ignored it, then they heard voices. At first, Laney thought she was dreaming. Her ears were intently listening, nose sniffing the air.

The voices sounded familiar and she ran over to the fence. She watched the couple approach and started to get excited. She could not believe what she was seeing. Could this really be her family?

They called, "Laney, Laney." In a second they were at the gate, running.

It was them!

Laney barked and ran to greet them. She was so excited. There were lots of hugs, kisses and a few tears. She always knew she would find her family and was so happy.

"I'm so lucky," she thought.

Later, everyone was introduced and stayed and visited. Molly and Laney played but always came back to the adults. Before Laney and her family left, Molly's mom invited everyone to a party the next day.

The party was lots of fun. The sheriff was there with Sadie. Charlie and Billy came. Molly's mom made peanut butter and honey pupcakes just for the dogs. All the dogs played, happy to be together.

Looking around at the group, Laney smiled.

All the adventures gave her new found confidence and she was very happy. Everything turned out differently, and better, than expected. She learned the forest wasn't so scary after all.

"Everything always works out when great friends are helping," she thought.

It was time to go. As she was leaving, Laney turned to her best friends,

"I'll be back soon and we'll have more adventures together."

Don't miss the next adventure!

Lucky Laney
Flames in the Forest

Somewhere in the high desert mountains.

....busily exploring new smells and playing chase, they failed to notice something flying above them.

Molly heard a quiet hum and looked up. Laney was also alerted. **"What is that?"** They wondered.

A small silver drone was circling the area above the dogs. It appeared to dip very close to Molly then dart away. Where Molly went, it followed. Its shadow and hum alarmed the dogs.

Someone, somewhere, was guiding it and seemed to be teasing them. **Why?** What were they looking for? Why were they following the dogs? **What did they want?...**

Made in the USA
Middletown, DE
04 June 2021